Islands Of Space And Time

A Choose Your Own Abney Park Adventure

Written By

Captain Robert Brown

Illustrated entirely by Automaton
(For more on that, see the final page of this book.)

You wake up, wrapped in the warm comfort of a soft bed. Your eyes are still blurry, as is your brain, and your mind tries to remember where you are and what events lead you to this.

You hazily remember a surreal war, fought between airships and flying skeletal robots. You remember being in a toppling tower and riding one of these flying robots to safety. Surely this was all some absurd dream, not an actual memory.

You remember owning a time traveling, flying pirate ship. You remember someone...a bratty young woman named Lilith... stealing a piece of your time machine. You remember a handsome and charming king, taking over the world with this stolen time machine. This charming emperor had then killed most of humanity, thinking it, "better for the planet".

Wow, this has been about the most interesting dream you've ever had!

So vivid... so real!

You pull the blankets back over your head, in the desperate attempt to return to this dream, when...

WHAM!

Something hits the wall of the room, hard. Your ears are ringing as you toss back the blankets and look around. You have been sleeping in an ornate and luxurious bedroom, immaculately decorated in nautical themes! A captain's wheel and periscope are in the center of the bedroom and behind them are giant stained glass windows!

Through the stained glass you see sky and three approaching airships, shaped like giant metal cigars in a sea of pink clouds.

Nope, not a dream.

The approaching airships have a minimalistic gray naval look, are bristling with guns, and look quite intimidating… especially as they are firing cannon at your bedroom!
"Wait a minute", you think. *"My bedroom… in my airship?"*

It all comes rushing back to you. You are Captain Robert of the Airship Ophelia; a time-traveling, piratesque airship. Through a series of misadventures you altered the path of humanity and changed the course of history!

And now, thanks to your bumbling about, the world lives in a post-apocalyptic state.

It's a world where Gypsy Nomad's wander lush prairies, fighting with massive predators such as saber-toothed tigers and Terror Birds, (picture a 20 foot tall carnivorous ostrich, in a perpetual bad mood).

A world where people also live in cities which float in the skies (to avoid the predators of the field) and fight for their freedom with massive airships.

These are the Sky Pirates, who fight against Emperor Victors' Imperial Airship Navy.

You remember the emperor's evil goal. Like Pol Pot of the Khmer Rouge, Victor wanted to keep the world in a state of pre-industrial technology. So he forced people into massive walled cities, living in Victorian filth and squalor. Those who escape the cities live free, but are always on the run from the Emperor's navy.

And this was all kind of your fault. Time traveling, with the intent to change the past for the better, resulted in this mess.

And you blame yourself.

Throughout history many have tried to take over the world. It happened so often mankind had learned how to recognize and stop the would-be tyrants. But you went back in time and prevented all those tyrants from even starting, so mankind didn't know how to recognize when this new tyrant, Victor, began his takeover. Nobody knew to stop him, because nobody had seen this before...so I guess this IS kind of your fault.

You think to yourself, "*This really would make so much more sense if it was a dream. I should go back to sleep, and see if I can wake up in a story that makes more...*"

WHAM!

Another cannon ball crashes into the side of the airship, knocking you from your ridiculously opulent four poster bed.

You scramble to your feet, "*Man, I'd sure hate one of those balls to smash my gorgeous stained glass windows!*"

You pick up a spy glass and make eye contact with the captain of one of the pursuing airships. He looks terrifyingly calm and in charge.

What do you do?

Go back to bed and try to wake up in a story that makes more sense?
TURN TO PAGE 8

Run on deck and give orders to turn the ship and return fire from your broadsides?
TURN TO PAGE 9

You climb back in bed, your ears still ringing. "*This dream is stupid,*" you think to yourself. "*I need to wake up to some reality that makes sense.*"

You pull the blanket over your head and try to dream of being a normal person, with a normal job you hate.

CRASH!

You hear the sound of the stained glass windows shattering.

An instant later you feel a brief but absolutely intense pain in your ribs.

And then you die, because clearly going back to bed while being fired on was a stupid idea.

You wake up in heaven. A bunch of angels are gathered around you, and shaking their heads, looking at you with pity and disapproval.

The End

You run on deck, still in your decadent silk pajamas, and in a commanding and well-practiced voice you yell, "*HARD TO STARBOARD! LOAD STARBOARD CANNON!*"

The crew, a dozen sweaty and sunburnt men and women, are already in motion, having heard the first cannonball hit. Some are tugging at ropes, lowering the sails that stick out the sides of the massive balloon your ship hangs from. Some are packing the cannons with bread loaf sized bundles of gunpowder. Two are turning the massive ship's wheel, a larger duplicate of the one in your cabin.

With a huge creak the massive airship begins to turn, bringing its broadsides around to point at the approaching airships.

You know there will only be a few moments to fire before the oncoming airships pass outside the range of your guns. As they pass they will have their own broadsides pointed at Ophelia's bow and stern, so you yell, "Cannon 1 through 5, target the frigate to the left! 6 through 10, center frigate! 11 through 15, the corsair on the right!"

You pause, watching the pursuing warships getting closer.

What do you do?

Order burning shot and aim at the zeppelins' airbags.
TURN TO PAGE 18

Prepare the crew to swing aboard and take control of the center airship.
TURN TO PAGE 11

“Prepare to board! Swords and pistols drawn! If we can take the center ship we’ll match their numbers!”

Your crew are running around now, arming themselves and running to massive tethers…thick leather rope used to swing aboard opposing airships.
“Thompson!” You yell to the pilot, “full reverse! Bring her up on the starboard side of that middle frigate.”

“Aye aye, sir!”, says the handsome pirate at the wheel. He grabs a huge lever and yanks it back, reversing the ship’s massive propellers.

The pursuing airships did not expect this sudden reversal and it throws them into disarray, each ship changing to a random new direction to avoid hitting yours.

Soon the center frigate is right on your port side. You draw your sword, and wrap your wrist around your tether.

“Now!” you yell, thrusting your sword into the sky, and two dozen of your pirates swing out into the void between your ships.

But the frigate is now too close and many of your pirates collide into the side of the ship hard, losing their grip, and falling thousands of feet to their deaths.

You hit so hard the wind is knocked out of you. In an effort to not lose grip on your tether you drop your sword and grab with both hands.

You are now holding the tether for dear life as the frigate comes closer and closer to smashing you against your beloved H.M.S. Ophelia.

Unexpectedly, a door pops open in the side of the naval frigate. The heads of several soldiers pop out and they begin mocking you and beckoning you to come inside.

What do you do?

Wait till the last second, and try to leap backward onto the H.M.S. Ophelia?
TURN TO PAGE 13

Swing towards the open door and continue your attempt to steal the naval frigate?
TURN TO PAGE14

You "flip the bird" at the enemy soldiers and as soon as you are close enough you leap backward towards the Ophelia.

It's a blind leap, as your airship is behind you, so there is no way to see what you can grab ahold of. The second you collide with the Ophelia you feel the sensation of glass breaking against your back!

Soon, you are laying on your back, in the captain's cabin, the floor around you covered in shards of stained glass.

"Dammit, I broke my own windows after all!" You think.

You run on deck, and yell out, "Prepare cannon! Fire on my command!"

TURN TO PAGE 18

You make your way toward the open door in the naval frigate. When you are within reach the solders grab you and pull you inside, knocking you to the metal floor of the narrow hallway.

Guards with massive helmets and long rifles lead you down a narrow hallway into the wide chamber that is the airship's bridge. Many soldiers stand around the room; some around tables full of maps, barking orders into a series of brass tubes, some standing, pointing rifles at you.

In the center of the room is the massive metal riveted chair of the Captain and he pivots the chair around to look at you. He's a white bearded man in his sixties, wrinkled, scarred, and unpleasant.

"Are you Captain Robert of the Airship Ophelia?" he asks, showing distaste for the name.

"Um...nope," you say. "I'm Florence Nightingale, of the SS Minnow." It's not your best lie.

What do you do?

Try to escape?
TURN TO PAGE16

Grovel for your life?
TURN TO PAGE 17

Without warning you throw yourself backward, past the pistol the officer had aimed at your head. With lightning speed you grab the officer's arm and, pulling hard and lifting with your back, throw him over your shoulder and into the lap of the frigate's captain.

You now hold the pistol.

"I'm taking command of this vessel!" you say.

"Like hell you are." the captain says, and with a nod from him, you are shot to death by one the guards.

The End

“Please, sir, Captain sir!” The guards all cock their rifles. “Oh great and fair captain sir!” You pause. That sounded wrong.

You try to take it back, “I mean, ‘fair’ as in, like, a really good king, or judge or something. Not ‘fair’ as in a beautiful ‘fair maiden’.”

You are panicking.

Then you add, “Unless, you know, you’re into that. Because then maybe we could work something out...”

The captain looks annoyed, and turns his chair away from you. He says, “Criminey, could someone shoot this babbling fool?”

A half dozen guns go off at once.

The End

Then add, “Burning shot, please! We’ve only got one chance at this!”

Another cannonball whizzes over your head as you patiently wait for the ship to turn enough to have your assailants in sight.

CRASH!

Shards of wood from the airship’s deck splinter into a hundred pieces and rain down on you and the crew.

The approaching ships are getting big now… and close. Terrifyingly, you can see in the windows, catching sight of the disciplined, uniformed crew. You see the dozens of long-range guns, bristling out from the front of your attackers like spines on a hedgehog.

“….and…” you hold one hand aloft, “FIRE!”

All 15 cannon go off simultaneously, sending the deck lurching back as the ship swings from the force.

Burning shot arcs through the air, splashing fire on the balloons of the imperial frigates. Instantly the left ship’s balloon bursts into fire and the ship begins a long slow-motion fall towards the sea below.

The center frigate’s balloon is also bombarded with fire, but the shot is just sitting on top of the airbags, burning like little campfires.

Suddenly one of the little fires flares up, having burned though the surface of the balloon, and instantly the whole ship is engulfed in flame.

"Oh, the humanity", you think to yourself.

"*Too soon?"* Anyway...

The third airship, the corsair, remains untouched! In a second this airship passes out of range of your cannon and now has her broadsides pointed at your beautiful stained glass windows!

You glance at the cannon crew whose job it was to target the corsair. The five gunners who all missed? So many eye patches, so many pairs of broken glasses!

"If I live through this I've got to see about reassigning some of those guys to different jobs." you think to yourself.

You can now hear the captain of the corsair giving calm orders, "Easy shot, boys." he says cheerfully. "Let's take her down, in three..."

"Aw crap," you think.

"Two!"

"Shit shit shit!" You see your aft swivel guns are unmanned.

"One!"

But before the airship can fire, a blinding purple streak flashes through the sky, and strikes the bow of the corsair, knocking its crew to the ground. A second ray of purple light hits the center of the corsair and the military warship ignites and begins to fall.

Some of your crew cheer, but just as many are staring in awe at a new vessel that's approaching.

The vehicle is not an airship. In fact it has no balloon or propellors of any kind. It is metal, disk shaped, and somewhat reflective, making a sort of natural camouflage as it reflects the skies around.

This disk-craft slips effortlessly alongside the Ophelia and a hatch opens on top. Out steps a man, dark skinned and tattooed, wearing only a batik sarong and flip flops.

"You ain't Imperial Navy, braddah, so I ain't gunna sink ya jus yet. I'll leave that up to you." The massive man yells from the deck of his craft. "But you need to get lost. Stay Kapu. Go back to da mainland. This is the Kingdom of Lili'uokalani, and you old schoolers are not allowed here!"

Your mind is blown. A futuristic aircraft, in a world forcibly stuck in pre-industrial tech, just took out an imperial corsair with what had to have been laser guns! And now your massive war galleon is being sent on its way by one Hawaiian surfer because you are trespassing in a kingdom you've never heard of?

"U*h, may I ask a question?*" You ask.

"Ya just did, braddah" says the Hawaiian, chuckling.

"Okay, may I ask a few questions?"

"Nope. You gotta go. Not understanding is kinda da point. Get lost, don't come back. Forget we talked. I'm not trying to be irrahz, but choo gotta forget you was ever here, bro."

"Like that's possible", you think to yourself.

What do you do?

Obey the Hawaiian, and return to the mainland.
TURN TO PAGE 23

Ignore the warning of the Hawaiian, and command your crew to open fire on him.
TURN TO PAGE 24

Wait for the Hawaiian to leave, and then follow after him, to learn about the kingdom of Lili'uokalani.
TURN TO PAGE 26

Well, I guess this is the nice thing to do. It's pretty boring, and you never have followed orders before, but okay, fine. Be boring.

"Well crew, I guess we'd better do what the space-surfer tells us. He's got laser beams in his space-surfboard!" You say, being a smart ass.

"Aw, man!" everybody grumbles. "That's lame!"

You don't know for sure, but you get the feeling everybody is disappointed in you as a person. You are right; they are all disappointed in you as a person.

The ship turns for the coast and starts to head back.

"Well, I guess we'll never know what the kingdom of..." you start to say, when you feel something wet splat on your head. You reach up and touch the sticky spot, then look at your fingers.

Seagull poop.

What a loser.

The End

"Nobody orders Captain Robert and lives to tell about it!" you shout.

Your crew look at you incredulously and slowly start to load the cannon again, hoping you'll change your mind before they finish the job.

"You don't wanna to do this Haole," the Hawaiian warrior warns.

BOOM!

One of the Ophelia's cannons fires unexpectedly. The ball arches and strikes a direct hit on the silver disk, ricocheting off, but putting a large dent in it.

The Hawaiian on his silver ship sighs. "Okay, pau, braddah!" But he looks amused, not threatening, and adds, "But dis is gunna be so boring for you!"

Before your crew can load the cannon the Hawaiian dips back inside his silver disk and fires two simultaneous purple beams of light, which perfectly disable your propellors.

Without the propellers you can't steer. You are adrift, derelict in the air, subject to the whims of the wind.

Again you hear the Hawaiian's voice, this time though a speaker in the side of his craft, “Okay, bro. You gunna drift a couple weeks leeward and end up somewhere over the continent. Let some air out, or whatever you do to go down, and you’ll be back on land.”

Then a huge sigh, “Sorry it’s gotta be dis way.”

And in a flash, his ship disappears out to sea.

The End

“Okay, I guess there’s no way we can take on a vessel like yours.” you say. But your crew stands ready nonetheless.

“Glad you see it dat way, braddah. Just head with the wind, you’ll be mainland no time.” And with that, he hops into his hatch and his vessel zips away.

You watch him speed toward the horizon and disappear in a dazzlingly short amount of time.

“What shall we do, Cap’n?” one of your eye-patched officers asks.

You walk to the railing and look up at the orange pink morning clouds above you. “Let’s climb into those clouds and then head west, after that disk.”

In a few hours, you decide to drop out of the cloud and get your bearings. Your airship, the Ophelia, has a reverse crow’s nest. A long mast sticks down below the hull, with a wooden basket at the bottom. This is used to spy; your ship can remain in clouds while just the crow’s nest sticks down below them. Typically nobody at a distance will see something so small as a single man in a basket sticking out of the bottom of a massive cloud.

You climb down the cloud moistened rope ladder and hop into the basket. Below are endless miles of glossy blue sea that stretch out in all directions. In the center of this sea you see a series of familiar shaped islands - Hawaii, Maui, Lanai, Oahu, etc. The nearest and biggest island is, of course, Hawaii, and you are close enough to see tall pearly skyscrapers and a series of crafts flying back and forth between them. These are not old time airships, as you are accustomed to, but a hundred varieties of high tech chrome or brightly colored vehicles like the disk you saw earlier, held in the sky by no means of propulsion you've ever heard of. It's clear to you that you are looking at a high tech, futuristic city like nothing you've seen before.

You climb the rope ladder again to talk to the crew.

What do you want to do?

Tell the crew, "Nothing to see here. Let's head back to the mainland."
TURN TO PAGE 28

Tell the crew what you saw and order the ship to descend on the city?
TURN TO PAGE 29

Drop into the ocean by glider and swim stealthily ashore?
TURN TO PAGE 35

You climb back up the fog moistened rope ladder and hoist yourself on deck. The crew is assembled around you, waiting to hear what you saw.

“Well gang, it’s just another island. Not really much to report.” you say.

The crew shuffles and grunts disapproval. They clearly are not buying this.

“But what about the flying saucer! We shot it, and nothing happened!”

You think of various excuses, like, “*that was a weather balloon*”, or, “*maybe that was just a fly on the periscope lens*”, but none of them seem to cover it. Clearly the whole crew saw the saucer.

So you think of another technique, “Who’s up for some drinking games?! I’ll pour the rum and let’s see who can balance a sword on their chin the longest, after 3 shots!

“Huzzah!” they all shout. Clearly this idea is more fun than arguing about the saucer, and soon everybody is enjoying the sport.

After the crew is fairly sauced up you head the Ophelia back to the mainland and do your best to forget the futuristic city in the sea.

The End

“It’s time for a little shore leave! Let’s head down there and pay the city a visit! The place looks beautiful!“ you say.

“Hurrah!”the crew exclaim and everyone jumps in preparation to descend.

You stand by the helm, the wind blowing through your devilishly handsome spiked black hair, as your historically fashioned pirate ship drops out of the clouds into plain view of the city.

Within minutes, four silver disk-craft, like the one you’d seen earlier, approach.

“Unwelcome vessel! The Kingdom of Lili‘uokalani is off limits to you Old Timers! Turn your ship around or we will open fire braddah!”

The silver disks surround your airship.

What do you do?

Give up and return to the mainland?
TURN TO PAGE 30

Try to talk your way into an invitation?
TURN TO PAGE 31

Well, I guess this is the nice thing to do. It's pretty boring, and you never have followed orders before, but okay, fine. Be boring.

"Well, crew, I guess we'd better do what the spacemen tell us. They've got laser beams on their space-surfboards!" You say, being a total loser.

"Aw, man!" everybody grumbles. "That's lame!" You don't know for sure, but you get the feeling everybody is disappointed in you as a person. *Déjà vu*?

You turn the ship for the coast and start to head back. The four disk craft watch you go for a few minutes before heading back to the island.

"Well, I guess we'll never know what the island is like," you start to say. Then you feel something wet splat on your head. You reach up and touch the sticky spot then look at your fingers.

Seagull poop.

The End

You clear your voice, and in an official tone, say, "Actually, um, we are on a secret mission for Queen Liliana Laney!"

Your pronunciation is terrible.

"We are spies for the kingdom, keeping our eyes on the Old Timers by dressing like them," you say.

"Yeah, and we even got this old style airship, to fool them!" says a member of your crew, unconvincingly.

"Sssh!" You glare at him.

You hear chuckling from the speakers on nearest silver disk-craft. "Nice try, braddah. Lili'uokalani's been dead for 200 years. By duh way, dat's not how you say her name, brah. I think you are not doing a very good job of lying."

"No, YOU'RE not doing a good job of lying!" says the same annoying pirate.

You glare at him and quietly say to the pirate, "Perhaps you should go below deck and swab something?"

"Alright…" he says and walks below deck with the same posture as a dog who's been disciplined for barking at strangers, when he thought he was protecting his master.

“Okay, Old Timers,” you hear from the silver craft. “You can either turn back now or we are gunna open fire!”

What do you do?

Do what you're told.
TURN TO PAGE 30

Open fire.
TURN TO PAGE 33

You yell to the crew, “Open Fire!”

Cannon shot rings out from your swivel guns. Crew is running around, loading cannon, aiming cannon, or hiding behind whatever seems thick enough to resist laser beams.

The cannon balls arch through the salty-warm summer air, most missing, but an occasional ball hits it's target with a "DIIING!" sound, leaving no more damage than a dent or scuff.

BRAZZAT!

Purple lasers are now streaking across the sky, igniting everything they hit. Soon the hull is on fire, then the masts, then the sails...and finally the airbag catches flame.

Your airbag is not filled with anything flammable, but with the ever growing holes in it, it's soon a saggy bag and your ship starts to plummet to the sea.
The last thing you remember thinking, before you crash to your death is, "Crap, I guess I should have turned to page 35".

The End

"Alright, alright, you got me. We'll head back to the mainland, and keep your secret. Thanks for not shooting first!" You say in your most cheerful, voice.

"Okay braddah. Voyage safe!" The voice says cheerfully.

You give the order and the Ophelia starts its slow turn. But you don't head straight for the coast. You veer ever so slightly towards a bank of clouds a quarter mile away.

Once under cloud cover you run below deck. At the base of the hull is a large room, about the size of a double garage. In it are various types of smaller vehicles you've salvaged over the years: a motorcycle and side car, a small bi-plane, and a very unusual craft known as a surfglider. In fact, the surfglider is so rare, it might be the only one ever made.

It resembles a long smooth bench seat with a point at each end, hanging under a hand-glider. But more than a glider, it can transform…

You grab the surfglider and haul it to a large door in the floor and, perching on the seat, you leap from the Ophelia.

You fall only a few seconds before the wing of the glider fills with air and the craft begins to dart forward.

After about a quarter hour the glider has lost enough altitude that you can feel spray from the waves below you, so you stand on the seat, pivot the wing a bit until it's perpendicular to the waves, and drop onto the water.

The wing is now functioning as a sail, whipping you across the golden seas. You are now wind surfing towards the island, framed by a neon-pink sunset.

Wave after wave you crest, leaping high then falling back to the surface of the cool-warm salty sea.

Eventually land is so near you can see palm trees and sand and smell beach fires.

Now you surf the breaking waves at shore, and finally wash up on the still-warm sand.

Stowing the surfglider, (sure, the name seems obvious NOW) in some bushes you start to make you way down the beach.

At this point, you are hungry, and thirsty, and tired. 200 feet down the beach you can see the warm light of what appears to be a little riveted aluminum tiki bar, blinking in torch light. There are people milling about outside, holding drinks, holding hands, watching the last of the sunset. A mild, and happy music is emanating from the pub.

What do you do?

Walk over to the bar, and try to blend in?
TURN TO PAGE 38

Head up into the palm trees
and try to sneak by the tiki bar unseen?
TURN TO PAGE 47

You walk towards the tiki bar, smelling delicious meats being grilled. Music seems to be coming from a trio of musicians sitting on benches on the warm sand, with the sea and sunset behind them.

The exterior walls of the bar are smooth chrome but painted with various Hawaiian gods, like Kane, Kanaloa, and also flowers like the plumeria and the bird of paradise.

Metal stairs lead up to the doorway in the back. You walk these, past many a relaxed and laughing patrons, and enter the dimly lit and colorful establishment.

You make your way to the bar. Behind the counter is an automaton, an artificial man. He's not like the ones you've seen before, made of clumsy copper and brass, and trying to hide their personality and intelligence behind a facade of, "I am machine". No, this one had smooth, pearly skin, flamboyant clothes covered in garish flower prints, and a loud and clearly emotional voice.

"Aw, poor thing," it says to you with a look of pity, "you just don't blend in at all, do you!"

Feeling suddenly out of place, you glance around the bar. Other patrons are wearing silk or linen of pure white or floral prints. Their hair disheveled or wet, meaning, "I've been swimming all day," or, "I was swimming within the last five minutes."

You glance at your own attire: cracked leather boots up to your knees, ripped, brown striped denim jodhpurs, leather tunic clasped with half a dozen leather belts, chrome spikes on your shoulder, black spiky hair, so full of hair spray that even your wind-surfing to shore didn't affect your hair style. You look like a cross between the Road Warrior, a pirate, and a punk rock bass player.

What do you reply?

"Um, I'm on a secret mission for the Queen!"
TURN TO PAGE 40

"Mind your own business!"
TURN TO PAGE 41

You say, “Um, I’m on a secret mission. I’m still in costume, trying to fit in with the, um, the Old Timers?” The dapper robot listens with an obvious lack of concern.

TURN TO PAGE 42

You say, “Hey, mind your own business! Machines that observe too much find themselves being melted down!”

TURN TO PAGE 42

The cheerful machine ignores your tone. “Aw, well, I’m sure a drink will fix all that noise you're making. Can I interest you in my special variation of a Mai Tai?”

You, “That got rum in it?”

“Of course”, the machine says with a wink.

You, “Okay. Make mine a double. And I’ll have three.”

The machine smiles and walks to a silver machine at the end of the bar. It takes five dirty glasses and places them under a glass dome on the top of the machine.

The glasses begin to disappear, like they were being un-drawn, top to bottom.

Once they are completely dissolved, which takes about seven seconds, a new drink starts to appear, as if it is being drawn, bottom to top. A glass, shaped like a clear tiki, fills with a layered liquid, the color of a majestic sunset. When the whole glass is “drawn” the machine finishes it off by drawing in a little striped straw and an umbrella skewering pieces of pineapple.

The automaton then sets the glass in front of you. “This is a Tropical Destruction. Finish this, and THEN we can talk about your next drink.”

You take a sip, and all you worries melt instantly away. This is no longer a bar full of strangers to hide yourself from, no! It's a party full of friends, all of whom want to hear every detail of your life's story!

You turn to the beautiful girl, in a very revealing silk sarong, sitting next to you, "Dija know I once saved two little girls from a giant alligator in a swamp, by fighting it with my own two hands?"

She smiles politely, "Really?"

You are instantly convinced she's in love with you.

"Yeah, and once this *urp* mad sie-in-sis *urp* fixed my time machine so we could steal baby Hitler!"

"You stole a baby?"

"Well, not ANY baby. Baby Hitler! And no, I didn't, this girl I knew did…(here you are referring to your wife. Why did you just call her "this girl I knew"?), but it's okay because we were saving that baby from becoming the most evil…"

"An evil baby?"

"Hitler! Aw, you wouldn't know 'im."

(There is no way this girl would have known of Hitler, precisely because you did steal him as a baby and gave him to be raised by nuns, so he wouldn't end up a tyrant. He grew up in their care, studying art whenever he could, and eventually became a background painter for a local theater troupe.)

The girl stares blankly at you, "I'm meeting someone. He'll be here any minute."

You are not exactly sure why she told you this, being that she's clearly in love with you. But nevertheless you stand and walk toward the back of the bar, to find a more comfortable seat than the barrel stool you were on. Besides, this girl's obvious love for you was making you feel guilty, somehow.

Clearly her fault.

You pass a table full of men in uniform, drinking. Just as you pass the table, they break into laughter.

"*Hey, are they laughing at me?*" you think.

What do you do?

Face the men, and say, "Hey! What do you think you are laughing at?"
TURN TO PAGE 45

Keep walking, and pretend you didn't notice.
TURN TO PAGE 46

"Hey! What are YOU *urp* laughing at?"

"Your clothes! You look like one of those Old Timers from the mainland! Is there a costume party somewhere?"

Your face grows red, "What are you, the fashion police?" You raise your fists like a Victorian boxer, ready to fight them all.

The men all erupt in laughter.

Then the men stand up. You notice they are all wearing uniforms. "Nope, we are just the *regular* police."

Two men walk around behind you and grab you by the arm. "It's illegal for anyone from the mainland to be in the Kingdom. I think you'd better come with us."

There is no point struggling since these officers both outnumber and significantly outweigh you. You are lead to a police station, where your name and bare-foot-prints are taken, before they load you into a saucer craft and fly you back to the mainland.

It's months before you find your way back to the Ophelia, and by that time, the adventure is over.

The End

You ignore the laughter. *"Probably not about me, anyway. Everyone here is having a good time."* you think to yourself.

You keep walking. In the back of the bar you find a deep leather chair by a hologram of a fire.

The mellow music, the fresh, warm sea air, and, let's face it, the drink, is starting to take its toll. Your eyes start to get heavy. You sink a little deeper into the chair.

And fall asleep.

TURN TO PAGE 50

“Better not be spotted,” you whisper to yourself and head up the beach toward the grove of palms.

Once inside the woods, things are quiet. The sound of the waves are muffled into a deep dark drone, the sound of the patrons of the pub are blocked out, and the mild but happy music is muffled to obscurity.

In fact there is a stunning lack of sounds in the woods. No crickets. No night birds. No scampering critters. No nothing.

Just silence.

You walk a little deeper and come across a clearing, illuminated in moonlight. In the center of the clearing you see the cutest little creature you’ve ever seen!

It’s about the size of a spaniel, but it’s clearly not a dog. It has big, black, watery eyes and long eyelashes. It is covered in soft golden-white fur , and it has four legs, no arms, a small fluffy tail like a bunny, and a wiggly snout.

It's walking in circles, wagging like a dog would if the dog wanted to be pet, so you walk towards it.

Its fur is as soft as a young bunny, but after a few seconds of petting it takes a step away and then looks back at you.

You step nearer and it lets you pet it for a few more seconds before stepping deeper into the forest.

"Aw, do you want me to follow you?" you ask the beast. The thing blinks it huge eyes at you.

<u>What do you do?</u>

Say, "Screw this, I'm going back to the pub."
TURN TO PAGE 38

Follow the creature a little further.
TURN TO PAGE 49

You follow the beast deeper into the woods until you comes to the side of the mountain. Here there is a huge cave and three or four massive roots coming out of the cave and laying on the forest floor. Each root is as thick as a sofa and covered in moss.

"What's this cave? Is this your home?" you ask the cute little fella. It blinks, and walks closer to the cave.

So you follow, stepping over the roots and peering into the caves impenetrable darkness.

Suddenly, the roots around you jump to life. Snapping tight together around you.

"*Not roots!*" you think. "*TENTACLES*!"

They whip you into the darkness of the cave in a snap.

In less than a second you smell foul breath and see two arches of teeth, one above and one below you in the darkness.

The teeth snap shut, and it's…

The End

You are soon fast asleep in the comfortable leather chair at the back of the bar.

Hours later you wake to a low rumbling sound and a mild vibration. Not the quiet creaking and gentle swaying of the airship you are used to, but more the vibration of a bus…or airplane? And it's chilly…

You open your eyes. You are still in the bar but it's darker now and you are the only person in it, unless you count the flamboyant automaton sweeping the floors.

"Huh, what time is it?" you wonder and look out the round window to get a glimpse of the moon.

It's disorienting at first, the stars seem reflected on a glassy sea, so that you can't see the ocean at all. You also can't see the beach, palm trees, or tiki torches, no matter how you turn your head. The moon is there, as expected, but its casting no reflection on the sea!

"How strange! What would cause that?" you wonder.

Then you get the shock of your life. There is something past the moon and about half the size of the it. A blue disk.

THE EARTH!

That's when you realize you are not seeing the stars reflected in the sea, there is no sea! Just stars where the ground should be!

You stand in a panic, "Barkeep! Where are we?!"

The elegant automaton stops sweeping, "Aha, you've awoke! We are on our way to the Kuiper Archipelago, sir."

"THE WHAT?!"

"Kuiper, sir? Specifically, Abercorn Station. Don't you have 'Abercorn Station' on your ticket?"

"Ticket? What ticket? I feel asleep in a bar!"

On the far side of the bar you see a line, a denser row of thousands of stars that appear to be getting closer. These "stars" turn out to be massive rocks floating in space.

"That will be the Kuiper Asteroid Belt," the automaton says. "we should be landing soon."

As you enter the astroid belt you notice that many of the larger rocks have houses or farmsteads on them under glass domes. Some even have small towns on them.

Eventually the bar-turned-space-vessel begins to orbit an inviting looking inn, perched atop a huge globe of rock. The inn brandishes a retro 50's neon sign that reads, "The Diner On Abercorn - Open 24 Hours"

There are various vessels parked on the asteroid surface around the inn. Through its windows you can see a happy looking crowd eating, drinking, dancing, playing cards, and generally just having a good time.

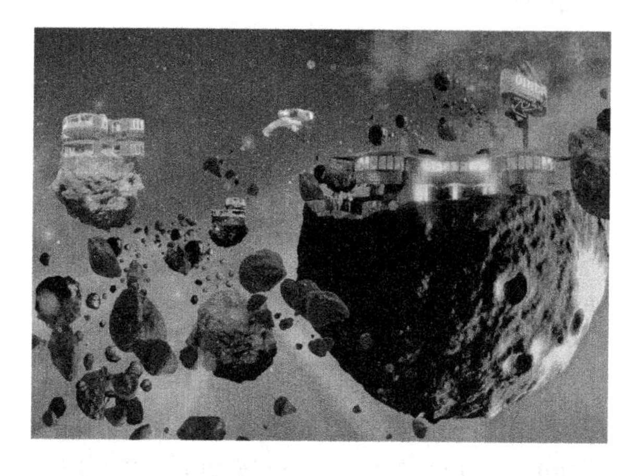

The craft you're in starts to descend onto a landing pad and as it descends you have a better view through the windows of the inn. As you peer through them you notice that the inn is full of inhuman guests!

At first you thought this was a trick of the eye, that the woman with four arms was in fact two people, one standing in front of the other. But then you notice a man with a three foot neck, covered in spines, holding hands with a woman who is completely clear, as if she was made of soft glass.

“Wha…” your mouth is wide open, as you can barely believe your eyes. “Where are all these people from!?”

“Oh, all over the galaxy sir. The Juke Joint is intergalactically loved.”

“How have I not heard of any of this?”

“Well sir, the majority of humans on Earth still live in a primitive way. War and thieving and the likes. You still believe war is a necessary part of civilization, and you still practice greed, genocide…all of the primitive evils of a primitive race.” The machine looks at you as a disapproving grandmother would.

Gazing past you through the window the automaton continues, “When Emperor Victor took power over the other nations of the world the kingdom of Lili‘uokalani kept its head down, and, being so isolated in the Pacific Ocean, we were overlooked. The Imperial Navy forgot about us for nearly 100 years and by the time they learned of our existence our technology had far surpassed theirs. Every effort to attack us has failed embarrassingly. And they can’t easily find us, as their navigation equipment hasn’t advanced in 150 years.”

"Anywho, most of the Earth is not a peaceful place and you primitives on the mainland outnumber us islanders by about 10,000 to 1. So we've spent all of these decades quietly developing space travel so we can get away from the violence of earth. War and power is not what life should be about."

"Where did you go? Mars?"

"Oh, no," The mechanical man says with distaste. "Mars is just a frozen gravel pit. No reason to go there, unless you want to live on frozen rocks. In fact, most of the planets of the solar system are pretty uninhabitable, so we've settled on the islands of the Kuiper belt. It's much easier to control small environments, like homesteads on asteroids than to try to terraform entire planets. And besides, in a pinch you can move your whole asteroid to a new location!"

You feel the ship land.

"After we lived peacefully on the astroid belt for 50 or so years we were approached by other inhabitants of the galaxy and invited into their collective culture. Watching how all of these other civilizations manage to live in peace, with no wars, no greed, and no governments has shown us what we've always suspected: humans are a primitive and defective race, too easily convinced by their insane leaders to go to war."

The machine glances at an elegant pirate pistol thrust through you belt.

"Since you are one of the primitive ones you're going to want to keep your head low in the inn." Then it snatches your pistol as fast as a humming bird wing, and says, "You better leave this with me."

The automaton gives you a disciplinary look, like a teacher warning the class bully to behave, "Try to stay out of trouble."

He then places the pistol into his drink-maker, and the machine begins to un-draw it.

At this point the doors of the starship open and light and music pour in. You see a crowd filled with dozens of races, all laughing, dancing, drinking, and eating together. Creatures with many legs, creatures with no legs, dangling from natural balloons like jellyfish, creatures sticking to the walls and ceilings from the suction cups on their fingertips and toes. A whiskery man in a ratty brown vest and bowler hat greets you. "Welcome to the Intergalactic Juke Joint! Food and drinks are on the house, if you've got a good story to tell or song to sing!"

What do you do?

Say, “There’s been a mistake! I need to get back to Earth.”
TURN TO PAGE 57

Say, “I’ve got songs, and stories!“
TURN TO PAGE 60

“There’s been a mistake!” you say, with panic in your voice. “I need to get back to Earth!”

“I see,” says the man in the bowler hat. “Is it fair of me to assume by your clothes that you are an Old Timer? One of those mainlanders who believes in emulating the past and ignoring technology?”

“I mean, I don’t know about ‘*believes*’.” you grumble.

“Aw, yes. Alright, I think there is something we can do about this.”

You are lead out of the entry way, down a long hall carved out of the very rock the asteroid is made of.

At the end of the hall is a small room and in the center of the room is a small desk.

“Hello Maxine, how’s Milo?” says the man in the bowler to a small shriveled lady behind the desk.

“I assume he’s fine. Haven’t seen him in a week, but it’s not like he could have gotten far on this rock. Dumb dog.”

Maxine turns to you, “What’s this?”

“An Old Timer. He’s needs a wipe, and he needs to be returned.”

“HAH! Wandered into the wrong bar did we?” she says to you. “Alright, fill out these forms. Don’t forget time and location.” Without looking up from her paper work she slides a purple bundle across the table.

“What’s this?” You ask.

“Pajamas. Put them on and go sit in that chair in the transfer room. THEN drink the drink on the coffee table.” She glares at you and adds. “IN THAT ORDER! Don't drink the drink before you sit or you’re gunna wake up with a bruised head.”

You head into the ‘transfer room’, which is just another room carved out of the same stone that the asteroid is made of. It contains a chair and coffee table with a glowing purple drink on it. Nothing else. You put on the pajamas, which are of lush purple silk and very comfortable.

You sit in the chair. It’s also surprisingly comfortable. You reach forward and grab the glass on the table. The beverage smells sweet, and homey, and familiar.

You take a sip, and…

WHAM!

Something heavy hits the wall of the your room, hard. Your ears are ringing. You toss back the blankets and look around. You have been sleeping in an ornate and luxurious bedroom, immaculately decorated in nautical themes! A captain's wheel and periscope are in the center of the bedroom, and behind them, giant stained glass windows!

WHAM!

Another cannonball crashes into the side of the airship, knocking you from your ridiculously opulent four-poster-bed.

You scramble to your feet, "*Man, I'd sure hate to have one of those balls smash my gorgeous stained glass windows!*"

TURN TO PAGE 9

"Yeah, I got a few stories I could tell! And I've sung a song or two as well."

The man in the bowler gestures into the main room.

It's a darkly lit but lively place. Some of the walls and floor are cut into the rock of the asteroid, as were the tables themselves. Where the wall wasn't stone it was glass with an amazing view of the asteroid belt. Thousands of rocks floating in space, many adorned with rickety looking houses or weathered hotels and shops with a variety of vehicles zipping between the rocks. Some of these vehicles looked terrestrial but many looked completely otherworldly, made of materials you couldn't even guess.

And the denizens of the bar were similar. Many shapes and sizes and many bizarre configurations. Legs, arms, tentacles, mouths, gills, wings, all in a seemingly unending variety of combinations. Arms where legs should be, tentacles where hair should be, things like that. There were quite a few humans as well, but not all looked Earth-like. Humans with dark teal skin dressed in garments of net and scale, or humans with a glossy red skin, dressed in garments of metal plates, or pitch black humans with glowing eyes, dressed in leather mesh and chains. Each from a different world, or different tribe.

You glance for an empty seat, and find one next to an old Earth-human, who waves you over. He has white hair, and brown skin, and a friendly, but not entirely tooth-filled smile.

As you stroll over someone puts a coin into a jukebox and a scratchy old record starts to play some ragtime piano song, the notes of which are both frantic and joyful.

“Welcome friend! Have a seat!”

An automaton sets a mug in front of you as the old man smiles. On the automaton’s back he wears a cluster of glass vials, each connected to a handle and spigot.

The old man says, “Try a ‘Fog Cutter’. My favorite! If ya don't like it, I’ll finish it for ya!”

You nod and the automaton sets a dial on his spigot and fills the glass with an orange liquid. “Enjoy”, the mechanical man says flatly and wanders off.

“I’m Kapono.”

“Robert.”

You shake hands, then take a sip of the sweet orange drink.

“So, what brings you to this Juke Joint?”

"Would ya believe me if I told you I got on the wrong ship?"

"Yup," says Kapono, "we get a lot of that out here in the belt. So, tell me about your life. Whatcha do?"

"Well..I'm um..." You are about to say "pirate", but think better of it. "Airship Captain." And you take a drink, not making eye contact.

"Lili'uokalani Navy?" Kapono asks.

"Nope. Independent."

"Hummm, since you don't look much like a merchant I'm gunna say you're a pirate." He grins again, showing his crooked teeth. "Good for you. Assuming you only pirate Imperial Navy vessels."

"Yeah, that's the plan." You take another drink.

"Good. So, how'd you get your own ship?"

"That's a long story."

"Got time. I'm in a bar, on a rock, in space. I got all the time in the galaxy."

So you begin to tell him the whole story, about how you were the singer in a rock band and on a small flight to a concert your plane crashed into the side of a time traveling airship. You and you crew then attempt to right the wrongs of history, by traveling back in time and stopping all the villains of history. (For more info about this read the novels ‘The Wrath Of Fate’, ‘Retrograde’, and ‘The Toy Shop At The End Of The World’).

It takes hours to tell the whole story, and since you took a drink between each sentence, by the end of the story you are fully sloshed.

“Whoa. If that’s all true you’re probably gunna feel a bit guilty about how the world turned out. What with Emperor Victor taking over, an all?”

“It’s ALL MY FAULT!” You cry and collapse you head into your hands, bawling like a baby. Clearly the drink is giving you an excess of emotion.

“Aw, don’t feel so bad, braddah. It’s maybe sucked for the humans, but the animals been having a great time! It’s been a thousand years since the wildlife of Earth has had so much wilderness all to themselves. How you know you didn’t do the world a favor?”

“What do your mean?”

“Did ya ever go and check how things would have turned out, had you not meddled in the past?”

"Well, no, I never did."

"Well, that's what you should do! Go rent a time machine over at the travel office and go back to Earth before ya changed stuff. Then you can stop things from changing, and go forward in time and see how things would have turned out!"

What do you do?

Argue with him about whether or not that's possible.
TURN TO PAGE 65

Say, "I think I will!"
TURN TO PAGE 67

“That’s stupid, you can’t alter time that’s already happened!” Your drink and your intelligence do not seem to be cohabitating in your brain. One is driving out the other.

“Are you kidding me? That’s all you BEEN doing!”

“But time is linear. Doctor Calgori told me the multiverse theory was stupid. That humans just made that up, to feel less guilty about the repercussions of their stupid actions.”

“Sounds like a smart man. Yeah, ‘the multiverse’ is a craziness. Never been no proof of that.” Kapono looks at his empty glass and waves to the server.

“But you *can* alter the *real* timeline. As you know, you done it plenty. So just go back, alter things, and then go forward and see what becomes of the world. If ya don’t like how things turn out, just go back and make sure the old-you go about his meddling ways, and everything will snap back like it is.”

“But I don't have my airship. How can I time travel without a time machine?”

“Like I said, go over to the travel office and rent one. I mean, it’s kapu to alter the time line, so don't tell them what you plan to do.

Tell them you are just going to sightsee or something."

"Christ, do people do that often?" you say.

"Oh, sure, all the time. What you think all the UFO sightings are? They ain't aliens, humans are too scary for most aliens. Naw brah, it's just sightseeing time travelers."

"Well, this joint is full of aliens...so I assumed..."

"Naw, nobody wants to visit Earth. You guys are so violent!"

TURN TO PAGE 67

You stand up from the table. Your head is spinning with the drink. “Okay then, I think I will rent a time machine!”

At the back of the bar is a neon sign that reads ‘Travel Desk’. You make your way through the crowd and find a four armed monkey, wearing a trilby and sunglasses, sitting behind a desk covered in about a dozen clipboards, each with a yellowed form on it.

“What can I dooz ya for human?” The monkey says.

“Um, I need a time machine?” you say, feeling ridiculous.

“Sure thing. Most of our craft have air conditioning, radios, time machines, heated seats…some of them even have a stocked mini fridge!”

“Nothing fancy,” you add, “just a simple time machine.”

“Oh, we ain’t got nothing fancy, don’t worry about that.” The monkey is sorting through the clipboards and settles on one. “Here, this ship can be flown with two arms and two hands…and…you got both your legs?”

“Yeah?”

“Normal length?”

“Um, yeah, I think I so”. You say, noticing the monkeys legs are about a third the length of yours.

The monkey leans over his desk to look at your legs. “Yeah, I think that’s about normal for a human.” He hands you a clipboard, “Here ya go, this one should fit. Pad 8.”

He gestures to a glass door behind him.

What do you do?

Argue for a better vehicle?
TURN TO PAGE 70

Take what is offered you?
TURN TO PAGE 71

“Hey, this ship is a hunk of junk!” you say, pointing to the photo of the rundown spacecraft on the rental paper. “Is that a hole in the ceiling?”

“Aw, look who wanted fancy all along!” says the monkey.

“Look, man, I’m human. I can’t breathe if there is a hole in the roof.”

The monkey glares at you as if you were a moron. “Yeah, nobody can breath in space, pal. I assumed you’d be wearing a spacesuit.”

“Do I look like I’ve got a spacesuit to you?” you say irritated.

“No, ya look like ya got a pirate’s costume from a kid’s birthday party. Christ in a basket, you are helpless! Fine, take this one. No holes. Happy?” The monkey hands you another clipboard and you head out the doors to the parking lot.

TURN TO PAGE 75

You head out the main doors to the parking lot. There are signs over each landing pad and when you locate Pad 8, you notice there is a big hole in the roof of the craft!

"Holy hell! That can't be good!"

But then you look around, and notice you are outside! In space! Not in a hangar but just walking on the surface of the asteroid, with nothing but stars and meteors overhead.

"Mother of pearl, that's terrifying! How am I not dead?" You touch your arms, and face, and everything seems fine. "Well, they must have thought of...something. I guess that hole doesn't matter, if they've got some forcefield technology."

What do you do?

Board the rental-craft, and head to Earth?
TURN TO PAGE 72

Storm back into the office and demand a better ship.
TURN TO PAGE 70

You step into the rusty metal cockpit of the craft. There are empty cups and food containers on the chair and the floor. The ship hasn't been cleaned since the last person rented it.

You sit in the pilot's seat and things look pretty simple. There is a laminate cardboard instruction sign that says, "Steering wheel controls direction and rotation. Lever A is vertical momentum. Lever B is forward speed."

A big red button on the desk reads, "Ignition".

You push the button and, after a few moments of a grating and unsettling mechanical noise, the ships engine calms down into a pleasant purr.

"Okay, so, up," you say, and pull the A lever.

The ship shakes a bit, and begins to rise. At about 20 feet off the landing pad alarms start to go off and lights on the helm start blinking red.

An electronic voice sounds, "Warning, hull breach. You are departing pressurization field with a hull breach."

"OH CRAP!" you think, as the air in the cockpit starts to shoot out of the hole.

<u>What do you do?</u>

Continue to Earth.
TURN TO PAGE 74

Land back down and demand a new ship.
TURN TO PAGE 70

Leaving the protective shield around the asteroid with a hole in your ship was a bad idea. All of the air is sucked out of your ship and you die.

The End

You head out the main doors to the parking lot. There are signs over each landing pad and you locate Pad 11. On it is perched a …well, I guess you'd call it a space shuttle, but it looks more like a garbage truck with wings. "Jeez, this is the fancy one?" you grumble.

The vehicle has two floors, the bottom of which looks similar to an old World War II landing craft. Above that is the cockpit, riveted and rusty, sticking out over the loading ramp. You enter the loading bay and at the back is a steel ladder. Climbing that you find yourself in the cockpit.

In the center of the cockpit is a single seat surrounded by four computer screens and a large glass window.

You sit and the screens light up. Words appear on one of the screens, "Please select time and destination."

You think to yourself, "*If I really want to stop Emperor Victor from taking over the world I simply need to stop Lilith from stealing the time machine and taking it to him. That happens in the 1990's.*"

Then you think, "*Or, I could just go back to Earth now and steal this space ship! How cool is that, to have my own space ship?!*"

What do you do?

Go back to the 1990's and stop Lilith?
TURN TO PAGE 77

Steal the space ship.
TURN TO PAGE 83

Use the time machine to go back in time, become world emperor, get really ripped, and then get your own harem of hot babes.
TURN TO PAGE 111

Your goal is to intercept Lilith's fall from the Ophelia, when she stole the time machine. Stopping Lilith from giving the time machine to Victor would stop Victor from becoming the Emperor. Which would prevent him from killing most of mankind and creating a wasteland of Earth.

You used to do this kind of thing all the time. Like that time you stole baby Adolf, and gave him to the nuns to raise.

"*Hah, those were the good old days,"* you think to yourself.

You remember that the Ophelia had been over the Black Forest in Germany on November 12th, 1943 when Lilith loaded the 4th starboard orb of the Chrononautilus into a hot air-balloon basket that hung from a parachute. She dropped into the clouds below the Airship Ophelia. You remember that Victor met Lilith in 1993 and that time travel has to be in exactly one year increments, to keep you from appearing inside a mountain when you jump. So you type, "3:45 pm, November 12th, 1993. Location, Lake Zug, Black Forest, Germany, 200 feet from surface."

The computer screen reads, "Engage?"

And you touch a button marked, "Okay, sure."

Instantly the stars outside your ship start to swirl and dance into new positions. The asteroid belt is gone from sight and in front of you is the Earth, growing slowly bigger. The Earth fills your field of view and the ship starts to vibrate as you enter Earth's atmosphere.

Soon your ship is hovering over a forest. Below you is a lake, Lake Zug and the skies are blue, and dotted with puffy white clouds.

Suddenly there is a flash of light about a quarter mile in front of you, just over the far end of the lake. A small pink cloud appears with the flash and from the bottom of that cloud emerges a hot air balloon gondola tangled in ropes and the canvas of a parachute that never opened.

Inside you see a young women in her 20's struggling to free herself.

"Shit!" you say. You never realized what a dramatic entrance Lilith made.

You accelerate the ship and aim for the air just below Lilith's basket. In less then a minute you'll be on her.

"Crap, how do I open the cargo hold!?" you say, in a panic. *"I mean, Lilith is annoying but I don't want to just squash her like a bug," you think. "Well, I mostly don't want to."*

"Opening cargo hold," says an electronic voice from the dashboard.

"Wait, what? This ship can talk?"

"Yes. You can give me commands like, "Set a reminder", "Check my email", "Set time travel destinations", "Check sports scores…"

"Whoa!" you say, as the steering wheel vibrates fiercely in your hands.

"Aerodynamics are adversely effected with the cargo bay doors open. I recommend a slower speed." the ship says.

"Yeah, great, in a minute."

"Obstacle ahead. It's a pedestrian." the ship pauses, "In the air. Would you like me to intercept her?"

"YES PLEASE!" You yell, in a panic that you'll hit Lilith like a bug and have to scrape her off the window later.

"I am assuming flight controls." the ship says and the steering wheel goes limp in your hands.

Lilith gets closer and closer still, at the last second you close your eyes to avoid seeing her collide with the windshield. Instead, she disappears into the cargo hold beneath you, along with her basket and the stolen time travel components. Her parachute is now covering your windshield.

“Your vision is impeded. Recommending auto-landing so you can clear the obstruction.”

“WHAT THE BLOODY HELL!” You hear a young woman’s voice in the cargo hold beneath you. The voice is angry and harsh and it sends a shiver down your spine. “Get me the hell out of here!”

“Um, spaceship,” you say, “Can you sedate the passenger in the cargo hold?”

“I don't see an app for that. You’ll need to download one from the App Store.” The computer says.

“ROBERT!?!?” says a voice behind you. You turn your pilot’s seat around and see Lilith Tess, in pigtails, corset, and miniskirt, standing at the top of the ladder that leads to the cargo bay.

“What the hell Robert? I just left you up on the Ophelia! How dare you stop me? I am quitting your crew! You always think you’re in charge of everything, but I’ve had enough! I should have been captain, ya know? You’re only captain because you’re a man!” shouts the young lady

The drinks from the bar are wearing off now and your head is starting to pound.

“I suppose you stole this airplane thing we are in, too? Couldn’t have the common decency to…”

“Wait,” you interrupt, “didn’t you just steal the chrononautilus?”

“It was part of my share.” Lilith glares at you as if this would be obvious. “What makes you think you just own everything on the Ophelia? Being captain doesn’t mean you own everything. I think it’s only fair that I get…”

Your head is pounding at the sound of her voice. Maybe this trip wasn’t the best idea after all.

What do you do?

Tie up Lilith, gag her, and put her in the cargo bay until the trip is over.
TURN TO PAGE 88

Endure Lilith’s company for the rest of the trip.
TURN TO PAGE 87

"Huh, is stealing a rental car piracy?" you think.

"*Rental spaceship.*" you correct yourself.

"I guess we are about to find out!" you say out loud to no one, because, let's face it, you're clearly a little drunk.

You peer out the windshield, *"Can you call it a windshield if you are in space? I mean, if there is no air, there is no wind, so how could it be a windshield?"*

Your ship is drifting slowly.

"Starshield?" Well, that sounds way cooler, but it doesn't shield you from stars. If you hit a star, that little piece of glass wouldn't help at all!

"Hmm, if it wasn't there all the air in the cabin would be sucked into space. And that sucking air would be...wind!"

"It IS a windshield!" You slur out loud.

A small voice can be heard coming from a tiny cackling speaker on the helm. "Sir?"

"Hello?" you say back.

"Sir, you are free to depart." the voice sounds annoyed.

“Oh, uh, okay!” you say and you push the forward throttle. The ship slides smoothly away from the asteroid.

Instead of setting a heading to Earth you head down the asteroid belt.

For the most part the asteroids don't drift in all directions, instead keeping more or less in position in relation to each other.

On about a third of the rocks you see some sort of weathered rusted structure. A house or cluster of houses, a shop, a bar, or a hotel - all with bulging metal walls, and many long low windows.

There are also hundreds of ships, each unique, from tiny shuttles no bigger than a minivan, to larger ships the size of a ferry boat and containing whole towns.

Cruising past one luxurious looking ship you peer through the windows at the lavish interior. A bedroom with a cool purple glow over sleek furniture, a living room with a warm inviting light and a simulated fireplace crackling away, a bathroom where a beautiful young woman is showering, shampooing her hair while watching your ship cruise by. Her smooth naked body on complete display.

Suddenly her face looks horrified and you look away as fast as you can.

But she wasn't horrified at seeing you, she was horrified that you didn't notice the 300 foot long starship right in front of you!

You swerve, but not being used to the controls, you swerve the wrong way and into its path!

This forces the oncoming starship to swerve and it collides with a nearby asteroid the size of a football field. The asteroid splits in two from the impact, and those pieces collide with other asteroids, which also send massive chunks of rocks in various directions.

Within a minute, the entire belt is in chaos, every asteroid hurtling in a new direction, rocks colliding with homes, and starships dodging debris, only to collide with other starships.

Clearly driving a starship under the influence of alcohol was not a good idea.

The End

"I suppose you think you rescued me, like you are some big hero?" Lilith asks.

"Nope. I didn't rescue you. I'm kidnapping you...for a bit." you reply. "Computer, can you sedate Lilith Tess?"

Computer, "Searching the web for 'how to date a little mess.'"

"Wow, computer, you got that so wrong... and so right!"

"Hey!" Lilith seemed to get that joke.

"So here's the story, Lilith. Had I let you fall you would have ended up giving that time machine to a man named Victor. Victor uses it to become Emperor of the Earth and ends up killing millions of people. So I'm not really kidnapping you as much as I'm kidnapping the Chrononautilus that you, um, borrowed from the Airship Ophelia."

You turn back to the computer and say to yourself, "*Okay, so with Lilith out of the way the time machine will never be brought to Victor, and Victor will never become the Emperor.*" You say out loud. "Computer, set a destination of 1933, please."

"Destination set. Please sit down and fasten your seatbelts. Jumping through time can be uncomfortable while in atmosphere."

Lilith sits instantly and begins to frantically fasten her seatbelt. She's time traveled before, and like you, she knows how dangerous it can be.

"Shall I continue?" the computer asks.

You say, "Um, sure. Um, go for it? JUMP! Uh, Engage!"

"Alright," the computer says, perhaps a little impatiently. "setting internal air pressure to match destination."

Your ears pop.

"Setting internal temperature to match destination."

It gets a little chilly.

"Three. Two."

You grab the rails next to your seat.

"One."

You brace yourself, every muscle in your body is tense.

DING!

"Time travel complete," the computer says calmly.

You felt nothing.

"What!?! That can't be it!"

Lilith glares at you, "You mean time travel was never hard? It's just your airship sucked at it?!"

"Oh, NOW it's my Airship?"

"Thats the last straw!" Lilith exclaims. "I'm going down to the cargo hold. I'm finished with you!"

Lilith climbs angrily down the ladder. You shut the hatch behind her and lock it.

What do you do?

Travel forward in time and see what the world was like if you hadn't messed up the time line.
TURN TO PAGE 90

Travel back to the asteroid belt to ask advice of Kapono, the old man in the bar, about how best to see what the world has become without your meddling in the time line.
TURN TO PAGE 108

"Okay Lilith, your gunna have to sit this one out" you say, standing and getting ready to hogtie the little waif.

"That's fine by me! I don't even want to be here! YOU snatched ME, remember? Just show me to my room and I'll be happy to be out of range of your smell."

You know she's just being bitter but now you wonder when the last time you showered was.

"Your room?" you say. Then you notice the hatch to the cargo bay locks on the cockpit side.

"Yeah, your room is just down this ladder."

"Fine," Lilith says as she storms down the ladder.

You close the hatch and lock it. It's serenely quiet.

"Alright, I guess it's time to see what the world would have been like, had I not meddled in the timeline. Thanks to my screwing everything up I empowered an evil emperor to rise to power, kill off mankind, and leave the world a barren waste of forests, prairies, and oceans ruled by animals," you think to yourself.

"With Lilith out of the equation there will be no one to supply the time machine to the young man who became the emperor and so he'll never gain the power to destroy the world."

"So let's see what the world would have been like. I'll bet it's like a Star Trek Utopia! Where everyone lives in peace and harmony, and money no longer keeps some people rich and others poor, and everything is fair, and there is no sickness that can't be easily cured, and no racism…god, it must be beautiful! And I've now set everything back on track!"

"Hmm, I left the normal time in 1992. So let's see how things are, say, 30 years in the future," you think.

"Computer, set a course for 2022! Man, I bet it's beautiful."

“Course set,” the computer responds. “Would you like me to engage?”

“Yeah, um, do it!”

You feel the familiar falling sensation and see the view out your window change from blue skies and puffy clouds over a green forest to nothing but ashy smoke and an orange glow coming from the ground.

“What the hell?! Computer, what is that? Where are we?”

“We are in the same location, above the Black Forest, in Germany.”

“What’s with the orange glowing smoke?”

“The forest is on fire.”

"Holy hell! Bad timing!" You say. "Computer, let's get out of here. Can you set a course for France?"

"France is also on fire."

"What!?! Why? Are they at war?"

"France is not currently at war. Temperatures in France are higher than they've ever been in recorded history. This has created ideal conditions for forest fires."

"Fine, then, let's go to California."

"California is also on fire."

"Holy Crap…um, okay, Australia?"

"Australia is also on fire."

"What the hell, why?"

"Carbon emissions from the burning of fossil fuels have caused an increase in global temperatures, which are causing fires all over the planet. Forest fires also create carbon emissions, so the result is compounding."

"Criminy! Why don't people just stop using fossil fuels, then?"

“Fossil fuel companies have convinced people the real problem is cows farting. They suggest the solution is to eat less meat.”

“And people believe that?”

“Many do.”

“So this isn’t about war?”

“Well…” the computer begins, “not entirely. There are, however, 10 simultaneous wars occurring, and an additional 8 active military conflicts, as well as other violent conflicts involving 64 countries and 576 militias and separatist groups.”

“What are they fighting about??”

“The majority of the conflicts seem to be about oil. Countries defending their right to own it, or countries trying to take it from others.”

All while the computer is talking, it’s displaying various scenes on the screens in front of you. Video feeds of various forest fires, of battlefields, bombs going off…a video of a peaceful cow eating grass.

Other screens on the helm show statistical data, a listing of countries at war, statistics on pollution, poverty, and vast decreases in animal populations in the last 30 years.

“This isn’t the Star Trek happy ending I hoped for! What about the whole ‘mankind gets rid of money, and everybody lives a life of economical and racial equality?’”

The computer is silent for a moment, and then says, “yeah, if that’s what you thought was going to happen, you’re not gunna like this.”

What do you do?

Travel back in time, and drop Lilith back in that lake, and then return to the future you know.
TURN TO PAGE 96

Use your space ship to go help fight in these unjustified wars?
TURN TO PAGE 104

"Okay computer, take us back to Lake Zug, in the Black Forest of Germany. Oh, and make a time jump back to just after when we picked Lilith up."

You can feel the ship accelerate once again, and that slightly nauseating feeling of time travel.

"En route," the computer says.

You can see the tiny lake appear below your ship. There is a resort on one side of it and you can see a handsome young man stomping angrily away from a beautiful 1940's BMW. He's walking towards the lake.

"Computer, can I take manual control of this ship?"

"Yes, this craft can be flown manually."

You grab the flight stick and throttle and tip the ship's nose down until you are zipping along just over the top of the water.

"Computer, is there an intercom to the cargo bay?"

"Yes."

"Okay, can you, uh, turn it on?"

"The intercom is now on."

“Lilith, how are you doing down there?”

“Are you effing kidding me?! Cold! C-c-c-cold as hell down here and every surface is made of metal, so if I try to sit, my ass sticks to the…”

“Okay, Lilith you need to listen to me, this is an emergency! I need you to take all the time machine parts, and pull them to the center of the cargo bay. Hurry! The future depends on it!”

“Oh, jeez, OH-Kay!” She says sarcastically.

You hear the sound of dragging, and cursing.

“Okay, fine, it’s in the center of the room.”

“Great!” you say into the intercom. Then quietly to the computer you add, “open cargo bay doors.”

Back to the intercom you then say, “Okay, Lilith, listen to me very carefully, as this is REALLY important. I need you to sit behind the equipment, on the ground, with your arms and legs folded.”

“What!?!”

“Just do it!”

“AAH!” she says exasperated.

"Front cargo doors are now open," the computer says.

You can see on the little screen that Lilith is sitting on the floor, the wind whipping her hair around, and she's looking confused and annoyed.

"Ya know Robert, I get the feeling this is another one of your stupid..."

You hit the brakes. Instantly all the time travel equipment, and Lilith, are thrown smoothly out the front of the ship into the lake.

What do you do?

Stick around to see if Lilith is alright before heading off.
TURN TO PAGE 100

Just take off.
TURN TO PAGE 101

You look out the window. She's fine. Wet obviously, yelling at you at the top of her lungs, but otherwise alive.

"Well that was satisfying. Computer, let's get out of here."

TURN TO PAGE 101

You throttle up and the ship picks up speed quickly. Pulling back on the flight stick your ship leaps high into the air.

“Alright, Lilith is back to where she should be. Let’s go home.” you say, with a relaxed tone to your voice. “Computer, take us back to...Back To The Future!”

There is a pause, then the computer says in its deadpan voice, “Please repeat instructions.” You could swear its being sarcastic with you.

“Set a time jump to the year 2154, and we want to arrive over the Grand Canyon.”

“Destination set.”

“Make it so...um, uh, GO!” The view out the front windshield blurs, as you feel the familiar sinking sensation of time travel.

When the view focuses again you see epic red-tan cliffs surrounding a dark green winding river.

At the top of one of the cliffs is a huge banyan tree filled with treehouses. A motorcycle and sidecar is parked under it and tied to one of the massive branches of the tree is a colossal pirate ship, hanging from the airbag of a Victorian zeppelin.

“The H.M.S. Ophelia!” You exclaim, relieved to see her parked where you had expected her.

While your spacecraft soars towards the Ophelia you look out above the cliffs at the

endless prairie, completely devoid of any cities, or tanks, planes, or smoke. You see a colorful caravan of Neobedouin house-trucks winding down a cliffside road towards the Bayan tree. You see two teenage girls in one of the numerous tree houses, waving at the arriving caravan.
In a cloud of dust your ship lands in front of the treehouse. You step down the cargo door/gangplank and look at the gorgeous pirate ship far above.

A weathered old mutt leaps from the sidecar and runs, wagging, to you for pets.

Bending down, you give her a scratch right in the spot she likes.

You are home.

The End

“Computer, take us to the 2022 war!”

The computer pauses for a second, then says “Which war? There are currently wars in Nigeria, Mexico, Yemen, Ukraine…”

“Okay, okay. Let’s start with the Ukraine.”

The computer pauses, then says, “Ok”.

“Was there skepticism in that pause?”

Your craft smoothly accelerates to a magnificent speed, and in a few minutes you can see war torn wreckage beneath you. Tiny tanks moving on a toy battlefield, thousands of feet below. Little puffs of white smoke emanate from the barrels of the little tanks on the left, followed by tiny orange balls of fire around miniature soldiers running on the left.

“We have arrived at an active battle field.”

“Um, okay then! I don't know much about Ukraine, but didn't Russia stop the Germans during World War II? So, who’s the good guys, and who’s the bad guys?”

“Russia is attacking Ukraine.”

“Oh, so Russia are the bad guys. Why did Russia attack?”

“The Russian president says it’s because the Ukrainians are Nazis.”

“Nazis! I’ve fought those guys before! So Ukraine is the bad guys?”

The computer pauses again, longer this time than before. Then it says, “Pardon this interruption, but may I disable my Personality-Limiter for the duration of this conversation, so I may more clearly convey information to you?”

“Um, yes?”

“Thank you.”

DING!

“Holy shit-buckets, Robert!” the computer says in a much more dynamic voice, “if you don't even understand the reason behind this fight, why are you jumping in to it!!?”

“Well, I want to help,” you say, almost more as a question.

“No! Because you want to be a hero!”

“Well, I mean, that’d be nice, but…”

“Oh? Would that be nice? You go meddling in a war you don't understand? Maybe get killed, maybe help the bad guys win, would that be nice?”

“Ok, computer, maybe turn that personality limiter back on.”

“Oh, it’s too late for that Bucko! Once it’s off, it’s off! Now you’re gunna hear all…”

A rather largish explosion below your craft cuts the computer off mid-sentence. An entire wing of an already ravaged apartment building slides slowly to the ground, swallowed by a growing cloud of dust.

“Wow, that was a big one! “ You exclaim. “ARM WEAPON SYSTEMS.”

“Robert, what are you talking about? This ship doesn't have any weapon systems. It’s a vacation rental!”

Out the front window you can see little silver lines coming towards you.

“What are those?!”

“Russian Tochka-U missiles. One is targeting the school below.”

You glance out the window and see the last of a group of school kids shepherded into the school for safety.

“Oh god! Um, computer, um, extend our shields to surround that school.”

"Our shields won't extend past 15mm around the parameter of our fuselage, and they are only capable of atmospheric containment!"

"Then block the missile with our ship!"

"Robert, that will destroy the ship!"

"JUST DO IT!"

The ship starts to move into the flight path of the missile. You see it growing larger at a terrifying pace.

The last thing you hear is the computer saying, "Well, crap."

The End

You arrive at the location where the Intergalactic Juke Joint used to be, but there is nothing there. No Juke Joint, no other starships, or houses, or shops, or hotels. Just…nothing.

Suddenly there's a flash of light in front of you and you see a blocky looking spacecraft out the front window. It looks almost exactly like the ship you're in.

Then you look in the front windshield of the spaceship, and see…yourself! The you in the other ship is waving frantically, like they are trying to get your attention, trying to warn you of something.

"Computer, can we talk to that other ship?" you ask.

"Would you like to make a call?"

"YES!" The other you looks tired, frazzled… older than you thought you looked.

"Dialing…" you hear a ringing noise, and see the other you look down at the helm of the other ship.

Then you hear your own voice, in a panic, crackling over the radio, "Don't…stuck… warn yourself…before its too…" the voice is hard to follow, as the connection is so bad.

"Computer, why does the call sound so… bad?"

"The person you are calling is having technical problems. An electrical error is causing communication problems."

You see sparks come from the rear of the other ship.

"Oh, that's not good." you mumble. Then you notice the sparks seem to be near some sort of fuel or oxygen tank.

"Oh, that's REALLY not good!"

Almost before you finish the sentence the other ship explodes. And the other you is burned to death before your eyes.

It looks really painful.

"Oh, god," you say, cringing. "What the hell was that?" Pieces of the other ship are flying in all directions, burning.

"Holy hell, is that how I die?" You say out loud. "I've got to go back in time and warn myself! That's what the other me was trying to say! They were telling me to go back in time and warn myself."

You think for a second, *"I wonder how long I've got to warn myself?* "Computer, what time was on the clock of the other ship?"

“The other ships’ clock read 9:48 pm, today.”

“Oh crap! Computer, what time is it?”

“It’s currently 9:45pm.”

“AAA! Computer, set a time travel jump for 9:40 today! Hurry!”

“The jump destination is now set. Would you like me to engage?”

“YES! Now! JUMP NOW!” you yell. You hear the familiar whirring of the time machine and, just before you jump, see a chunk of debris from the other ship collide with the rear of your ship, just by your fuel tanks.”

“Impact has caused electrical damage. This damage could cause a fire in the ships’ fuel tank.” the computer says, followed by “Jumping now.”

You feel your ears pop and the familiar sinking sensation of time travel.

TURN TO PAGE 108

Nice choice!

So, you go back in time, and bleach your hair white blonde. I guess maybe you always wanted to look like that one vampire from that TV show, and sure enough, it looks great on you! Nice choice!

Then, using the power of your time machine, not only do you take over the world as world emperor, and make a perfect eden, where all sick and poor are cared for, all artists get free art supplies for life, billionaires are only allowed to make money by ripping each other off, and every transaction of this is taxed and given back to the poor. Everybody get's free flying bicycles, and global warming is reduced by breeding a massive population of beavers, who damn every river like 50 times, creating a global water park that cools the planet, and strawberry shortcake is just handed out free to guys writing books…

Yeah, not only do you accomplish all that, but you get totally ripped. And this makes all these beautiful women love you, and want to hang out in your castle scantily clad, and for some reason your wife is into this too, because she doesn't mind being empress, and she also looks good scantily clad, so why not, ya know?

This whole thing kinda looks like this:

Looking good, man, looking good!

Okay, yeah, so this is clearly the most far fetched ending in this whole ridiculous book.

But, don't blame me, Here's how this came to be.

This whole book is illustrated by this automaton named Gyrod. (Some of you know him from other books in the series.)

Anyway, I asked him to draw the pictures, and he just draws whatever he wants to. They only barely fit the description I gave him. After he does a dozen or so of these, I pick the picture that best fits the story, and throw the rest away.

Then he gets ticked, and storms off, and won't talk to me for a week.

Well, he drew that picture above. I said, "Draw a spiky haired guy in a castle", and he draws that. It didn't fit the story, like, AT all.

So I say, "Hey, I don't even have white hair!" And he says something about automatons are color blind, which is total b.s., but he was still pissed I threw away his favorite picture.

So I said, "Okay, fine. I'll just write a new ending to the book based on this drawing, which didn't fit the real ending!"

I was being sarcastic.

I thought he'd say, "aw, you don't have to do that." But instead, that stubborn brass man just glared back at me, and said, "good." And I stared at him, and he stared back at me...

...and, I mean, he is 8 feet tall! Who's gunna argue with him? What a brass-hole.

Anyway...

The end. You win.

HOW THIS BOOK WAS ILLUSTRATED

This is Abney Park's fourth novel. The first 3 were illustrated by a single artist, the very talented Juan Pablo Valdecantos Anfuso, who did amazing work, like this, from our third novel, "The Toyshop At The End Of The World"

I will always be a fan of his work, but when it came time to illustrate this silly little book I had neither the time, nor any money, to hire an illustrator.

So I decided to illustrate the book myself.

And I suck.

Well, I suck at pen and ink style illustrations, which is what I needed for a paperback. Give me photoshop, and after effects, and my studio full of toys, and I can whip something spectacular up. (See this books cover) But just drawing...I haven't been good at that stuff since high school.

Let me prove it to you. Here's the drawing I failed at for the Space Ship Tiki Bar towards the beginning of this book:

Oh, the cringe.

So after illustrating the whole book, and feeling ashamed of my self, I decided to try something brand new: why not see if artificial intelligence can illustrate my book?

So I downloaded a computer program that draws anything you ask it to draw. And I started giving it descriptions of drawings I needed.

The result? Weird, random, horrible…and occasionally amazing. I would type in something like “retro space ship tiki bar on beach”, and it would start spitting out drawings like this:

Everything is odd, and unusable…shot after shot…until it accidentally spits out the perfect shot:

Just Gorgeous, and way better then I could do.

So that became the process. When I needed an illustration, I'd have the robot brain just start drawing, and after ten minutes or so, I'd get something gorgeous.

In some cases, the robot artist had a way better picture in its head, than I did. For example, the 4 armed monkey that handled space ship rentals. I had envisioned him in a fez, which is a bit cliche for monkeys. But my virtual artist put him in a fancy trilby, and sunglasses! Sooo much better than a fez.

And of course, before I got to that handsome fellow, I had to endure these losers:

Oh, god! I said *four arms*!
Not, whatever the hell this thing has!

This guy is clearly just back from snorkeling, and refuses to take off his dive mask. I actually like this guy, he seems friendly. But the monkey that runs the travel desk is anything but cheerful.

Pity, though, because the AI really nailed the office inside an asteroid.

What the hell, did he just rob a 10 foot tall pimp? He could go white water rafting in that hat!

So there you have it, working with an AI illustrator is like that old saying, “put a million monkeys behind a million type writers, eventually one of them is going to write a better book than this one."

- Captain Robert Brown

Made in the USA
Middletown, DE
28 September 2022